The Best Easter Hunt Ever

by John Speirs

Cartwheel
·B·O·O·K·S·®
SCHOLASTIC INC.
New York   Toronto   London   Auckland   Sydney

To Siggy, Tilly, Rolly, Alexandra, and John

ISBN 0-590-95624-8

Copyright © 1997 by John Speirs.
All rights reserved. Published by Scholastic Inc.
CARTWHEEL BOOKS and the CARTWHEEL BOOKS logo are registered trademarks of Scholastic Inc.

12 11 10 9 8 7 6 5 4 3 2 1   7 8 9/9 0 1 2/0

Printed in the U.S.A.   24

First Scholastic printing, February 1997

How to Use This Book

These children are going on an Easter hunt.
You can, too. Use the rebuses.
Look for the hidden Easter treats in the colorful pictures.
On a sheet of paper, keep track of how many Easter treats
each child finds — Roy, Sara, Tina, Alexis, John, and you.
Who finds the most treats?

The answers to the puzzles are on pages 26-31.

The excited children wake up early to begin the best Easter hunt ever.

Sara finds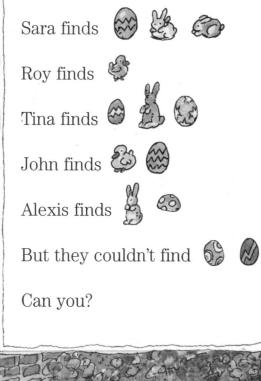

Roy finds

Tina finds

John finds

Alexis finds

But they couldn't find

Can you?

They race to the garden.

Sara finds

Roy finds

Tina finds

John finds

Alexis finds

But they couldn't find

Can you?

They run along the country lanes.

Sara finds

Roy finds

Tina finds

John finds

Alexis finds

But they couldn't find

Can you?

Next they walk through the village.

Sara finds

Roy finds

Tina finds

John finds

Alexis finds

But they couldn't find

Can you?

The school yard is a great place to look for treats.

Sara finds

Roy finds

Tina finds

John finds

Alexis finds

But they couldn't find

Can you?

The children look along the riverbank and across the bridge that leads to town.

Sara finds

Roy finds

Tina finds

John finds

Alexis finds

But they couldn't find

Can you?

They hurry through the busy streets.

Sara finds

Roy finds

Tina finds

John finds

Alexis finds

But they couldn't find

Can you?

Searching far and wide,

Sara finds  🥚🥚

Roy finds 🥚🥚🥚

Tina finds 🥚🐤

John finds 🥚🐰🥚

Alexis finds 🐰

But they couldn't find 🐿

Can you?

They go on to the fair where lots of Easter treats are waiting.

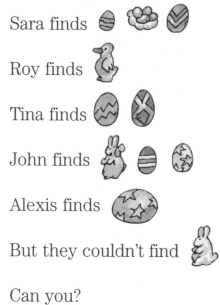

Sara finds

Roy finds

Tina finds

John finds

Alexis finds

But they couldn't find

Can you?

What fun to look along the
boardwalk!

Sara finds

Roy finds

Tina finds

John finds

Alexis finds

But they couldn't find

Can you?

Home again—
just in time for an Easter party!

Sara finds

Roy finds

Tina finds

John finds

Alexis finds

But they couldn't find

Can you?

Answers

pages 4-5

pages 6-7

Answers

pages 8-9

pages 10-11

Answers

pages 12-13

The school yard is a great place to look for treats.

Sara finds

Roy finds

Tina finds

John finds

Alexis finds

But they couldn't find

Can you?

pages 14-15

The children look along the riverbank and across the bridge that leads to town.

Sara finds

Roy finds

Tina finds

John finds

Alexis finds

But they couldn't find

Can you?

Answers

pages 16-17

They hurry through the busy streets.

Sara finds

Roy finds

Tina finds

John finds

Alexis finds

But they couldn't find

Can you?

pages 18-19

Searching far and wide,

Sara finds

Roy finds

Tina finds

John finds

Alexis finds

But they couldn't find

Can you?

Answers

pages 20-21

They go on to the fair where lots of Easter treats are waiting.

Sara finds

Roy finds

Tina finds

John finds

Alexis finds

But they couldn't find

Can you?

pages 22-23

What fun to look along the boardwalk!

Sara finds

Roy finds

Tina finds

John finds

Alexis finds

But they couldn't find

Can you?

Answers

pages 24-25

Home again—
just in time for an Easter party!

Sara finds

Roy finds

Tina finds

John finds

Alexis finds

But they couldn't find

Can you?

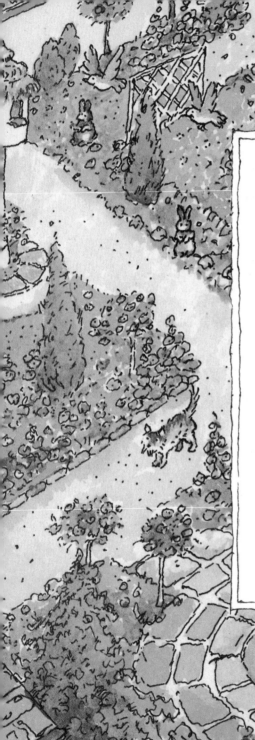

Sara found 24 Easter treats.

Roy found 25 Easter treats.

Tina found 21 Easter treats.

John found 23 Easter treats.

Alexis found 19 Easter treats.

Did you find 14 Easter treats?

Roy is the winner!